DATE DUE		

International Organizations

Save the Children

Jennifer Nault

WEIGL PUBLISHERS INC.

Published by Weigl Publishers Inc.
123 South Broad Street, Box 227
Mankato, MN 56002
USA

Web site: www.weigl.com

Library of Congress Cataloging-in-Publication Data

Nault, Jennifer.
  Save the Children / Jennifer Nault.
    p. cm. -- (International organizations)
Summary: Presents the history of the international Save the Children
organization, discussing its origin, mission, goals, and achievements and
providing some related human interest stories.
Includes bibliographical references and index.
  ISBN 1-59036-021-4 (lib. bdg. : alk. paper)
  1. Save the Children International Union--Juvenile literature.
[1.Save the Children International Union.] I. Title. II. Series.
  HV703 .N35 2002
  362.7'06'01--dc21

                                        2002006563

Printed in Canada
1 2 3 4 5 6 7 8 9 0   06 05 04 03 02

Credits

Project Coordinator
Michael Lowry
Copy Editor
Diana Marshall
Photo Researcher
Gayle Murdoff
Design and Layout
Warren Clark
Bryan Pezzi

Photo Credits

Every reasonable effort has been made to trace ownership and to obtain
permission to reprint copyright material. The publishers would be pleased to have
any errors or omissions brought to their attention so that they may be corrected
in subsequent printings.

Cover: Howard Davies/Exile Images; **AFP/CORBIS/MAGMA:** page 27; **Neil Cooper:** pages
22 bottom, 23 top; **Corel Corporation:** page 18; **Howard Davies/Exile Images:** pages 3, 5, 6,
21 bottom, 22 top; **Bill Gentile/CORBIS/MAGMA:** page 13; **Robert Maust/PHOTO AGORA:**
page 15; **Sean Sprague/PHOTO AGORA:** pages 11, 25; **National Archives of Canada/PA-
168131:** page 21 top; **Save the Chilren Fund UK:** page 7, 20; **Ursula E. Seeman/South
Florida Sun-Sentinel/Corbis Sygma/MAGMA:** page 19; **Skjold Photographs:** page 24;
UN/DPI Photo/152390c/J.Issac: page 9; **UN/DPI Photo/153554/J.Issac:** page 26; **UN/DPI
Photo/187401C/P.Sudhakaran:** page 23 bottom; **Waterpartners International:** page 14.

Contents

What is Save the Children?

Save the Children is an international nonprofit organization that helps children in need in about 120 countries, including the United States. Unfortunately, there are many children who require a helping hand. This is the story of volunteers from across the globe working together to create opportunities for children who need their help.

Save the Children believes that all children have rights. Young people deserve a happy, healthy, and safe start in life. However, many children are born into poverty. They suffer through wars and natural disasters, such as drought and earthquakes. Poor health, disease, violence, and **discrimination** are endured by millions of young people. Save the Children works to help such children. The organization creates and supports many programs. It works to improve education, health care, agriculture, and economic standards. Save the Children provides **sustainable** solutions to many of the problems that affect the world's children.

Save the Children also has a political presence. It works with governments on policy changes that will benefit young people.

> "There is much work to do, and when nearly a billion children go to bed hungry, neglected, or abused every night, we cannot wait."
>
> **Charles MacCormack, President of Save the Children U.S.**

Save the Children supports practical projects that allow children to improve the quality of their own lives.

Quick Fact • • • • • • • • • • • • • •

Save the Children U.S. helps young people in Ethiopia by delivering millions of gallons of emergency drinking water to drought-stricken areas.

Just the Facts

Founded: In 1919, the Save the Children Fund was formed in the United Kingdom. In 1932, Save the Children U.S. was founded in New York City.

Founders: Sisters Eglantyne Jebb and Dorothy Buxton founded the very first Save the Children. In the United States, Save the Children was founded by a group of concerned citizens led by John Voris.

Mission: To give children a healthy, happy, and safe start in life, and to provide sustainable solutions to the problems children and communities face worldwide.

Number of member organizations: Thirty-two

Scope of work: Save the Children works in nineteen states across the United States and in about 120 countries around the world.

An Organization is Born

Save the Children is an umbrella organization, which means that there are many different branches around the world. The first Save the Children organization was the Save the Children Fund, which was formed in England on May 19, 1919. Since that time, Save the Children has grown into a network of thirty-two member organizations. In the United States, Save the Children has been active since the 1930s, working on behalf of children in the United States and overseas.

> **"Save the Children provides communities with a hand up, not a handout."**
>
> **Save the Children U.S.**

The founders of Save the Children in England started the organization because they were concerned about the treatment of children in Germany and Austria. During World War I, only limited supplies of food and other provisions were reaching Germany because of blockades. As a result, some children living in Germany and Austria were starving to death.

Two sisters brought attention to the suffering of the German and Austrian children. Eglantyne Jebb and Dorothy Buxton knew they had to take action—and fast. In 1919, Eglantyne met with other concerned citizens in London, England. Immediately, they began sending food to the German and Austrian children.

In January 1932, a group of U.S. citizens built on the successes of the British organization. They formed Save the Children U.S. to respond to the needs of families suffering in the United States as a result of the **Great Depression**.

Approximately 600 million children on the planet live in poverty. Save the Children believes all children have a right to a happy, healthy, and secure start in life.

PROFILE

Eglantyne Jebb

Eglantyne Jebb was a remarkable woman who worked tirelessly to protect children's rights. She was born in 1876 to a wealthy family in Shropshire, England. As a child, Eglantyne was strong-willed but caring. Eglantyne became an intelligent young woman. In 1895, she began her studies at Oxford University. An excellent student, her favorite classes were the political sciences. When Eglantyne graduated from university in 1898, she trained as a teacher. At the time, it was unusual for someone with Eglantyne's background to become a teacher.

In 1899, Eglantyne began teaching at a liberal school in southwest England. Eglantyne's students loved her, as did the staff. Still, she felt that there were other ways that she could help children.

"We need to place in children's hands the means of saving themselves."
Save the Children's Founder Eglantyne Jebb

In 1903, Eglantyne began charity work. She wrote a book about helping the poor. In the book, she proposed education and local development as solutions to poverty. Ten years later, Eglantyne visited the Balkans, a region of southeastern Europe. Eglantyne was greatly shocked by starving children in the Balkans and the horrible effects of World War I on German and Austrian children. She was determined to help. With the assistance of her sister, Dorothy Buxton, Eglantyne created the Save the Children Fund in 1919. Three years later, Eglantyne wrote a paper on children's rights called the Declaration on the Rights of the Child. It listed five basic rights that a society owes its children. It proved to be a radical document.

Eglantyne died of a stroke on December 17, 1928, at the age of 52 years. Friends and volunteers were determined to keep her vision alive. Today, the Eglantyne Jebb Society and Save the Children organizations around the world continue the work that Eglantyne Jebb began.

The Mission

The work of Save the Children is based on promoting the rights of the child worldwide. In 1923, Eglantyne Jebb drafted a special **charter** for children's rights. It was the first charter in the world to address the rights of children. The charter stated that children were entitled to a good quality of life. It also stated that governments and adults were responsible for providing children with basic human rights.

The Declaration of the Rights of the Child changed the way children were viewed on a global scale. It also served as the basis of the 1989 United Nations Convention on the Rights of the Child. This convention declared that the protection of children's rights is a matter of international law. Almost every country in the world has signed the declaration.

Save the Children believes that everyone shares the responsibility of helping children in need. This responsibility is shared across the globe. Today, the International Save the Children Alliance, which is the name given to all the Save the Children offices worldwide, is the largest organization dedicated to helping young people in the world.

In 1999, Save the Children celebrated its eightieth anniversary. The organization continues to fight for children's rights in the twenty-first century.

> "Today, Save the Children is still at the forefront of promoting children's rights—particularly their right to have a say on matters that affect them."
> **Save the Children UK**

Quick Fact

Children's rights are set out in the United Nation's Convention on the Rights of the Child. This document took ten years to create. It includes input from different countries, religions, and cultures.

Throughout the developing world, nearly 90 million school-aged girls do not have access to primary education.

The Declaration on the Rights of the Child

The principles in this document remain a guiding force for the organization today.

• The child must be given the means to develop normally in all ways— morally, spiritually, and materially.

• The child who is hungry must be fed; the child without a home must be sheltered; the child who is sick must be nursed; the child who is mentally or physically handicapped must be helped; the **maladjusted** child must be re-educated.

• The child must be the first to receive relief in times of distress.

• The child must receive training, which will enable him or her, at the right time, to earn a livelihood, and the child must be protected against every form of **exploitation**.

• The child must be brought up with the knowledge that his or her talents should be devoted to the service of others.

Key Issues

Young people face a wide variety of challenges. The International Save the Children Alliance has identified key areas where it works to enhance the lives of children.

Health

The goal of Save the Children's health-care programs is to make real and lasting improvements in the health of children, families, and communities. Save the Children's programs bring sustainable improvements to health care around the world. Save the Children has targeted several key health issues.

1. The reduction of infant and newborn mortality

Every year, 4 million babies die before they reach 1 month of age. Four million more babies are stillborn. About 98 percent of these deaths occur in **developing** countries. Often, there is no doctor available to help mothers when they are giving birth. Many babies could be saved if appropriate health care was provided. Underweight or sick newborns also require special health care. In 2000, Save the Children U.S. launched a global program devoted to helping mothers and newborns. Called Saving Newborn Lives, this program is dedicated to keeping newborn babies alive.

2. Health care for birthing mothers

Every year, more than 500,000 women die during pregnancy or childbirth. Save the Children works in developing countries to bring proper care to mothers in need.

3. Health-care resources to children in school

Disease and a lack of proper nutrition affect children the world over. Vitamin deficiencies, **malaria**, and **AIDS** are just some of the health problems that affect children. Save the Children offers many programs that bring nutritional and health services to children in schools worldwide.

Quick Fact • • • • • • • • • • • • • • • •

In sub-Saharan Africa, 173 out of every 1,000 children die before they reach the age of 5. By comparison, in developed countries the death rate is 6 per 1,000 children.

Every year in the developing world, more than 6 million children die as a result of malnutrition. One of the major goals of Save the Children is to prevent child hunger.

The International Save the Children Alliance states that:

- children have the right to be protected from violence and abuse

- children have a right to be healthy and well educated

- children have a right to speak out, telling adults what they want and what they expect

- children have a right to join in the decisions made about their own futures

Poverty

One child out of every four lives in poverty. A person living in poverty does not have enough money to adequately clothe, shelter, or feed himself or herself. Poverty means that children have very few opportunities to improve their lives. Save the Children is dedicated to solving child poverty issues. The organization believes that every child should have an equal opportunity to improve his or her quality of life.

Save the Children UK aims to cut child poverty in half by the year 2015. This is an ambitious goal since more than 600 million children survive on less than $1 a day. In North America, that is the price of a bag of potato chips. Save the Children battles poverty by investing in community development and providing debt relief to countries that are struggling economically. It is also working to eliminate user fees for services such as health care and education so that they are available free of charge.

Child Labor

Poverty is one of the main causes of child labor. There are about 120 million children between the ages of 5 and 14 years working full-time. Another 130 million children work part-time. Save the Children makes it a priority to talk to working children to find out what they need. The organization funds after-hours schools for working children and drop-in centers where children can seek advice and obtain health care. Save the Children meets with companies that employ children. In doing so, it encourages the employers to act responsibly. Many children are physically abused at work and are made to work in unsafe conditions. Save the Children works to protect these vulnerable children.

Education

Today, 128 million children worldwide do not attend school. Without access to education, it is very difficult for these children to improve their lives and prepare for the future. Many children who do not attend school go without supervision during school hours. Mothers are often forced to leave their children alone all day while they work. Save the Children tackles education issues in about fifty countries. It works to provide basic education for children, as well as out-of-school educational programs for those children who are unable to attend a regular school.

Quick Fact ••••••••••••••••••••••••••

Save the Children U.S. gives direct assistance to schools, such as the school in Taluk Tasarm, Thailand. Many children in Taluk Tasarm are forced to work at an early age, so Save the Children lobbied to make attendance at local schools compulsory until Grade 6. Now, most of the children stay in school until they graduate. Save the Children U.S. also offers after-school classes in music, dance, and sports to children living in Taluk Tasarm.

CASE STUDY
Dennis Hernandez

Some children who live in the poor districts of Tegucigalpa, Honduras do not have access to basic education. Some of them cannot afford the enrollment fee, supplies, or uniforms that are required to attend school. These children do not have the chance to improve their lives through education. Twelve-year-old Dennis Hernandez lives and goes to school in Tegucigalpa. He teaches children in the community who cannot afford to go to school.

Dennis organized a group of young people who did not have enough money to attend school. He decided to teach others the things he was learning every day at school. He wanted to help the children who did not have the same opportunities as himself.

Dennis feels changed by the experience. He has learned to understand other people—especially other children. Dennis wants to continue teaching the young people in his area. He will continue to give lessons and help children in need. Eventually, Dennis wants to become a doctor.

> "Children feel more confident being among other children. We understand each other better, we joke and talk, and each person can give their opinion. Children tell me what's bothering them, and I try to help and give advice."
> Dennis Hernandez

In Dennis's community, Save the Children UK helps train children to become educators. The organization also provides training to children in health and children's rights issues. The hope is that these children will, in turn, help other children.

Discrimination

Throughout the world, children are often ignored, face discrimination, and are denied basic human rights because they are young. Save the Children strives to make children's voices heard. Girls are especially subject to discrimination all over the world. Girls often have less access than boys to education and health care. Girls are a special focus for Save the Children's efforts.

Children with physical disabilities are particularly in need of protection. Quite often, these children are mistreated or are left to fend for themselves. Usually, these children are the last to receive proper care and education. Children who cannot walk sometimes go without wheelchairs because they are not available in their community or they cannot afford to buy one. Young people who are blind often have few educational resources to meet their special needs. Save the Children offers training and medical services to communities who need assistance.

Community Development

Children need to live in safe and productive communities. Save the Children works to help communities become self-sufficient by supporting local improvement efforts. Save the Children puts particular emphasis on **famine** prevention. It also supports the building of safe water and sewer systems. Through these actions, it aims to reduce incidences of water-borne diseases, malnutrition, and famine in the future.

Access to safe drinking water and adequate sanitation are the most important factors in fighting disease in the developing world.

CASE STUDY
Drought in Ethiopia

Ethiopia is ranked among the poorest countries in the world. Since 1999, crop failures and drought have left many Ethiopians struggling to find enough food and water to survive. More than 8 million people, half of them children, face starvation.

Save the Children U.S. was the first international agency on the scene to report the extent of the severe drought in 1999. The organization has been working in Ethiopia since the 1930s, when Save the Children established its first child welfare center in Ethiopia. Since then, the organization has helped many people by delivering food, water, medicine, and training programs to communities in Ethiopia.

One person who has benefitted is Endrias. Endrias is 15 years old. He lives near the town of Akesta, in northern Ethiopia. The area depends on rainfall during March and April to grow crops, but no rain has fallen for several years. Endrias's town has experienced severe food shortages and poverty as a result of the drought. Save the Children U.S. has brought in food and distributed it to the people in the area. It provided aid to Endrias, his family, and many others living in Akesta.

Today, Save the Children U.S. remains stationed in Ethiopia. It is working to prevent future food shortages. It monitors the areas in Ethiopia that frequently experience food shortages and trains local farmers to help re-establish food security.

> "When I get hungry I feel tired, and then when I eat I get a stomach ache. I play with my friends to forget I'm hungry, but I just watch them when they play football, because I don't have the strength to play."
> Endrias

Around the World

Since Save the Children was formed in England in 1919, branches in many other countries have been created. The International Save the Children Alliance is an association of independent, non-profit, voluntary organizations. It supports children, families, and communities throughout the world. Today, there are thirty-two alliance members that strive to make a difference in about 120 countries.

Countries with Save the Children organizations are colored in yellow on this map.

ICELAND
Barnaheill

CANADA
Save the Children Canada

UNITED STATES OF AMERICA
Save the Children U.S.

DOMINICAN REPUBLIC
Fundación para el Desarrollo Comunitario

MEXICO
Fundación Mexicana de Apoyo Infantil A. C.

GUATEMALA
Alianza para el Desarrollo Juvenil Comunitario

HONDURAS
Asociación Salvemos los Niños de Honduras

ARGENTINA
Save the Children Argentina

FRANCE
Enfants et
Developpement

UNITED KINGDOM
The Save the
Children Fund

NETHERLANDS
Save the Children
The Netherlands

DENMARK
Red Barnet

FAROE ISLANDS
Barnabati

NORWAY
Redd Barna

SWEDEN
Rädda Barnen

FINLAND
Pelastakaa
Lapset Ry

LITHUANIA
Save the
Children Lithuania

ROMANIA
Salvati Copiii

MACEDONIA
Save the Children
of Macedonia

N

JAPAN
Save the Children Japan

KOREA
Save the Children Korea

HONG KONG
Save the Children
Hong Kong

FIJI
Save the
Children Fiji

GREECE
Save the
Children
Greece

ITALY
Save the
Children Italia

SPAIN
Save the
Children Spain

JORDAN
Jordanian Save
the Children

EGYPT
Egyptian Save
the Children

MAURITIUS
Save the Children
of Mauritius

SWAZILAND
Save the
Children
Swaziland

AUSTRALIA
Save the Children
Fund Australia

NEW ZEALAND
Save the Children
Fund New Zealand

U.S. Operations

Save the Children provides relief to children in economically developed countries, such as the United States, as well as developing countries. A strong economy does not mean that a country's children are not at risk. In the United States, many children suffer from domestic violence and neglect.

About 5 million children in the United States are left unsupervised when they are not in school. Often, this is because their parents have to work. Save the Children U.S. and a group of other organizations work together on a program called Save the Children Web of Support. This program provides 125,000 young people in 18 states and 240 communities with safe environments, caring adults, and educational activities during their out-of-school time. These programs give young people the opportunity to improve their reading skills, graduate from high school, foster a healthy lifestyle, and acquire community leadership skills for the future.

> "I choose to support Save the Children because I believe in their work and the positive impact they have in communities around the world."
>
> **Roma Downey, Save the Children Sponsor**

Approximately 16 percent of children in the United States live in poverty. The child poverty rate is estimated to be nearly three times higher than other industrialized nations.

CASE STUDY
Fund for U.S. Children in Crisis

Save the Children U.S. responded quickly to the needs of children in the United States after the terrorist attacks on September 11, 2001. The organization established the Fund for U.S. Children in Crisis to offer counseling and support services to children who were affected by the attacks. Children living in some of the lowest income communities, including those in the New York City area, were helped. Often, these children do not have strong family support. They require extra help from volunteers in times of crisis.

Over $1 million was donated to the Fund for U.S. Children in Crisis. The money was allocated to provide resources in many areas. For example, immediately after September 11, Save the Children U.S. contributed $10,000 to the New York Times' 9/11 Neediest Cases fund. This money was used to help some of the victim's families.

The money from the fund was also used to provide other community programs for children, parents, and educators. Children in the Save the Children after-school programs were given access to counselors. Parents, teachers, and community leaders were provided with age-appropriate resources to help children cope with the events of September 11. Save the Children also organized forums to help children learn and practice cultural and religious tolerance.

The Fund for U.S. Children in Crisis is part of the Save the Children Web of Support program. As well as funding after-school programs and education forums, this support program manages a Web site for teenagers called Youth NOISE.

Teenagers were able to chat online to other teens about their feelings after September 11th. The Web site also helps young people find ways to help others and provides information on current issues.

Milestones

The different organizations in the International Save the Children Alliance have been helping children throughout the world for more than eighty years. Since 1919, Save the Children has provided assistance to children in times of war, famine, and other hardships.

1930s: International Expansion

The Great Depression sweeps across the nation in the 1930s. This is the worst and longest economic collapse in the history of the modern world. It lasts from the end of 1929 until the early 1940s. Save the Children U.S. responds to the needs of poor children living in Appalachia, in the southeastern United States.

1919

A fundraising campaign led by sisters Eglantyne Jebb and Dorothy Buxton is the first step toward the formation of the Save the Children Fund, also known as Save the Children UK. The money raised helps children living in war-torn Germany and Austria.

1920

Eglantyne Jebb forms the International Save the Children Union. It is composed of organizations from different countries dedicated to helping children in Europe.

1921

Save the Children UK responds to a famine in Russia by feeding as many as 650,000 children.

1920s: Focus on Children's Rights

In the 1920s, Save the Children UK begins to publish books about its international work. With Eglantyne Jebb's Declaration of the Rights of the Child as its main focus, it starts new relief programs. These include providing meals to starving children in Russia. Save the Children's efforts help save many children from dying of starvation.

1922

Save the Children UK gives money for child **refugee** relief in Albania through the International Save the Children Union.

1923

Eglantyne Jebb writes the Declaration of the Rights of the Child. The intention of the document is to make people realize the importance of protecting children's rights.

1923

Save the Children UK opens feeding centers in Greece. It provides food for about 47,000 Greek orphans. These children are refugees from the war between Greece and Turkey.

1940s: World War II

The work of Save the Children UK in Europe is greatly disrupted by World War II. Save the Children is forced to withdraw many of its projects. In the UK, Save the Children begins searching for solutions to social problems caused by the war. Housing projects and nurseries are established to shelter child refugees. Day care is set up for the children of parents working in wartime industries.

1945–50

Relief work continues for refugees and displaced children in Europe. This leads to the establishment of day care and medical centers in Greece, Yugoslavia, Austria, Italy, and West Germany.

1947

In Germany, Save the Children UK begins running hospitals and orphanages for displaced children. Most of the work is concentrated on the settlement of refugees from East Germany.

1948

A blizzard hits the southwestern United States. Save the Children U.S. offers relief and school sponsorships to Native-American children and their families.

1950s: A Different World

The situation in Europe begins to return to normal after the war. However, there are still many displaced families and children. The Save the Children Alliance continues to work in Germany, Austria, Italy, and Greece. It also continues its work outside Europe in Africa and the Middle East.

1952

The Queen of England becomes the **patron** of Save the Children UK.

1955

Save the Children UK sells its own Christmas cards to fund its projects and to raise awareness. By 1955, sales of these cards reach 100,000.

1924

The League of Nations adopts the Declaration of the Rights of the Child.

1930

The Save the Children Fund gives a grant to India to teach local women how to be better **midwives**.

1931

Save the Children UK provides money to purchase an orphanage in Estonia. It serves as a home and school for Russian refugee children.

1932

The United States branch of Save the Children is founded in New York City.

1936

An International Save the Children Union delegate, Frieda Small, sets up the first child welfare center in Ethiopia. It includes a feeding station for malnourished children and an infant medical clinic. The work is partially funded by Save the Children UK .

1956

During the Hungarian uprising, Save the Children UK sends emergency relief and sets up children's homes.

1959

The Declaration of the Rights of the Child is adopted as part of the United Nations charter.

1960

When an earthquake hits Agadir, Morocco, Save the Children UK sends emergency supplies and sets up medical clinics in the area.

1961

Save the Children UK opens its first refuge for Tibetan children in India.

1963

Dorothy Buxton, co-founder of Save the Children UK and sister to Eglantyne Jebb, dies.

1966

Projects begin in Vietnam for orphaned, injured, and refugee children affected by the ongoing Vietnam War.

1960s: Facing New Challenges

In the 1960s, Save the Children UK forges new relationships with governments in developing countries. Some projects begun by Save the Children are handed over to local organizations, while others are managed jointly. Save the Children continues to protect the rights of children, including Tibetan refugees, children in Vietnam, and children harmed by the civil war in Nigeria.

1970s: A New Face and New Directions

The International Save the Children Alliance is founded. The Alliance combines the Save the Children International Union, founded by Eglantyne Jebb, with several Save the Children organizations in other countries.

1980s: Decade of Empowerment

Save the Children UK has operations in about fifty countries. It increases its efforts to help children w are starving in Ethiopia.

1971

Bangladesh asks for Save the Children UK's assistance. This marks the beginning of long-term health, nutrition, and community development operations in the region.

1974

Save the Children UK begins work in Latin America after a hurricane hits Honduras. This is the beginning of the development of long-term health and nutritional programs for children in Latin America.

1975

Save the Children UK sets up a nutritional project in Papua New Guinea.

1976

Guatemala experiences a terrible earthquake in 1976. Save the Children Norway responds by sending emergency supplies, and

1990s: Approaching a New Millennium

Wars continue to affect children all over the world. Most notably, wars in this decade are fought in Iraq, Sudan, Somalia, Mozambique, Nicaragua, Colombia, Sri Lanka, and Sierra Leone. Save the Children UK helps to create a law aimed at ending the use of child soldiers. Save the Children UK also works in Eastern Europe, providing aid to children in the Balkans. The organization begins to emphasize children's own power in the creation of change.

2000: A New Millennium

In the United States and the United Kingdom, Save the Children's dedication to young people is now bolstered by its dedication to improve the lives of mothers. The organization's efforts to improve the education and health of mothers helps ensure that their children will be given the support and care that they need. Save the Children U.S. is also providing economic support to mothers. With the support of Save the Children U.S., mothers can create their own small businesses and become self-sufficient. The organization continues to tackle global problems such as hunger and unsanitary living conditions.

1990

The first Save the Children field office opens in Ghana.

1992

In Cambodia, Save the Children Norway expands many of its projects. It works to improve children's nutrition and to prevent child exploitation.

1994

In Afghanistan, Save the Children U.S. provides health education and funds basic education. It offers training in children's rights and conducts research on homeless children.

1999

This year marks the eightieth anniversary of Save the Children UK.

2000

President George W. Bush visits Bridgeport, Connecticut and offers his praise for an after-school program supported by Save the Children U.S.

2001

In response to the terrorist attacks in New York and Washington, DC, Save the Children U.S. establishes the Fund for U.S. Children in Crisis.

begins long-term development programs in the country.

1979

Save the Children UK launches the Stop Polio Campaign in its attempt to end polio worldwide.

1980

Save the Children UK begins a large famine relief program in Karamoja, Uganda.

1983

Save the Children U.S. and Save the Children UK begin a massive emergency relief program for people affected by famine in Ethiopia and Sudan.

1986

Save the Children U.S. works in Thailand to support orphanages and provide assistance for children with physical disabilities. It also works to give students, especially girls, secondary education or job training.

Current Initiatives

Save the Children U.S. continues to support children in local communities across the nation. The after-school program at the South End Community Center in Bridgeport, Connecticut, offers educational, cultural, and recreational classes. The program, called the Get BUSY (Building Up South-End Youth) Collaborative, offers a range of after-school and summer activities to about 175 children aged between 15 and 19 years. About eighty children attend the center's program on any given day. Save the Children runs similar after-school programs in Brooklyn, New York.

> "Innovation and experience has been the key to Save the Children's success."
>
> **Save the Children U.S.**

Save the Children works toward creating the conditions in which all children have the opportunity to develop to their full potential.

Quick Fact • • • • • • • • • • • • •

The United States has yet to sign the United Nations' Convention on the Rights of the Child. The only other county that has not signed the document is Somalia.

CASE STUDY
Girls Education: Strong Beginnings

Save the Children U.S. runs an international campaign called Girls Education: Strong Beginnings. It believes that educating girls in developing countries is one of the best ways to invest in the future. Save the Children U.S. supports initiatives to keep girls in school. Working with local communities, the organization promotes early school enrollment and the continued education of girls. It also lobbies for educational reforms.

In many parts of the world, girls must complete many daily chores and tasks. Often, this work keeps them from attending school, or makes success in school difficult. Girls who begin having babies at a very young age are less likely to receive a complete education. In some areas, people do not think that girls need an education. Sometimes, a family's religion will dictate that the girls stay at home. Save the Children is working to reverse practices that discriminate against girls.

At any one time, there are many wars being fought in the world. Some of the people most affected by war are children, who usually depend on adults to protect them from harm. Every day, more than 5,000 children are forced to move from war zones. War does more than just threaten children with physical danger. During conflicts, children may be separated from their families, become orphaned, or be exposed to abuse and neglect.

Some children even participate in armed conflicts. More than 300,000 children under 18 years old are currently involved in wars acting as soldiers, minesweepers, spies, or porters. A child may become involved for many reasons, such as family poverty, the need for protection, or because they have been abducted.

Save the Children believes that children should not be used in war under any circumstances. It works to help children living in war zones such as Uganda, Mozambique, El Salvador, and East Timor. When young people become separated from their families during a war, Save the Children helps reunite them. As well as distributing emergency aid, the organization works to reduce the emotional and physical damage children experience in times of war.

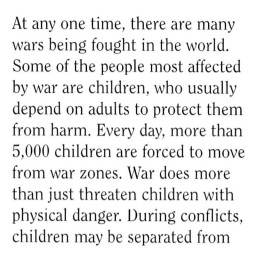

In Afghanistan, an average of four children are injured by land mines every day. More than 30 percent of the 100,000 land-mine victims are children.

CASE STUDY
Mohd

Mohd Ismail is a young boy who is the president of the Children's Committee for Village Development. Mohd lives in a small village in India. In 1999, soldiers from Kashmir targeted the village. After that, it was occupied by the Indian army. Mohd experienced many terrifying events.

Mohd was at school when the shelling started. All of a sudden, there was total confusion. Children were running around looking for their parents, and parents were running around searching for their children. The young students could hear the sounds of guns booming close by. The teachers told them to run toward their homes. The schoolchildren did not even have a chance to gather their shoes and books—they just ran.

As a result of the destruction, the villagers were brought to Kargil, where they stayed for three months. The children were homesick. They felt even worse when they found out that their homes had been destroyed.

> "The army left a lot of dirt and litter around—even some unexploded bombs. The committee decided to clean up the village. There was also a bit of water pollution, so we decided to go to the source of the stream and clean it."
> Mohd Ismail

When the villagers returned home, there was nothing left in their houses. Soldiers had taken everything. Some houses had been blown up. At the village school, the furniture had been smashed, and the science laboratory was completely gone. Nothing was left behind. Mohd felt very sad about what had happened to his community.

The village had much rebuilding to do. Mohd contributed to the decision-making process by becoming president of the Children's Committee for Village Development. The committee was able to repair the school with the assistance of Save the Children UK. During the repairs, Save the Children set up a winter school and provided students with fuel for warmth. It also gave the young people warm clothes. Mohd plans to become a doctor, so he can help the villagers just as Save the Children helped him.

Take Action!

Become an active and responsible citizen by taking action in your community. Participating in local projects can have far-reaching results. You do not have to go overseas to get involved. You can do service projects no matter where you live. In fact, young people are helping out every day. Some help support overseas projects. Others volunteer for projects in their home communities. Here are some suggestions:

Anyone can get involved in improving the lives of children around the world. You can start by helping to raise public awareness in your own community. If you feel strongly about an issue that affects children, write a letter to your local newspaper. Writing a letter to the editor gives you a chance to have your voice heard. People often write letters to the editor to discuss views and opinions on current issues. This increases public awareness, which often results in action. Save the Children knows how important it is to raise awareness.

Those of you who want to be really active can raise funds to sponsor a child through Save the Children. This enables you to make a difference in his or her life. Sponsoring a child means sending them money through Save the Children. You do not have to be a sponsor on your own. Organize a few friends or classmates together to share in the monthly cost of sponsoring a child. Your money helps provide the child with beneficial programs and services. When you sponsor a child, you begin a relationship with that individual. Sponsors receive letters, photographs, and drawings from their child. They see firsthand how their help is making a difference in a child's life.

To find out more about sponsoring a child, surf to the following Web site: www.savethechildren.org/childsponsorship1.jsp

Where to Write

International	United States	Canada
International Save the Children Alliance 275–281 King Street London W6 9LZ UK **UNICEF** Palais des Nations 1211 Genève 10 Switzerland	**Save the Children U.S.** 54 Wilton Road Westport, CT 06880 **United States Fund for UNICEF** 333 East 38th Street New York, NY 10016 **The National Center for Missing and Exploited Children** Charles B. Wang International Children's Building 699 Prince Street Alexandria, VA 22314	**Save the Children Canada** 4141 Yonge Street Suite 300 Toronto, ON M2P 2A8 **Kids Help Phone** 439 University Avenue Suite 300 Toronto, ON M5G 1Y8 **UNICEF Canada** Canada Square 2200 Yonge Street Suite 1100 Toronto, ON M4S 2C6

In the Classroom

EXERCISE ONE:

Make Your Own Brochure

Organizations such as Save the Children use brochures to inform the public about their activities. To make your own Save the Children brochure, you will need:

- paper
- ruler
- pencil
- color pens or markers

1. Using your ruler as a guide, fold a piece of paper into three equal parts. Your brochure should now have a cover page, a back page, and inside pages.
2. Using your color markers, design a cover page for your brochure. Make sure you include a title.
3. Divide the inside pages into sections. Use the following questions as a guide.
   - What is the organization?
   - How did it get started?
   - Who started it?
   - Who does it help?
4. Summarize in point form the key ideas for each topic. Add photographs or illustrations.
5. On the back page write down the address and contact information for Save the Children.
6. Photocopy your brochure and give copies to your friends, family, and classmates.

EXERCISE TWO:

Send a Letter to Your Congressperson

To express concern about a particular issue, you can write a letter to your member of congress. This can be an effective way to make the government aware of issues that need its attention. To write a letter, all you need is a pen and paper or a computer.

1. Find out the name and address of your congressperson by contacting your local librarian. You can also search the Internet.
2. Write your name, address, and phone number at the top of the letter.
3. When addressing your letter, use the congressperson's official title.
4. Outline your concerns in the body of the letter. Share any personal experiences you may have that relate to your concerns. Use information found in this book to strengthen your concerns.
5. Request a reply to your letter. This ensures that your letter has been read.
6. Ask your friends and family to write their own letters.

Further Reading

Freedman, Russell and Lewis W. Hine (photo.). *Kids at Work*. New York: Clarion Books, 1998.

Kielburger, Craig and Marc Kielburger. *Take Action: A Guide to Active Citizenship*. Toronto, ON: Gage Learning, 2002.

Kielburger, Craig and Kevin Major. *Free the Children: A Young Man Fights Against Child Labor and Proves that Children Can Change the World*. New York: Harper Perennial, 1999.

Kuklin, Susan. *Iqbal Masih and the Crusaders Against Child Slavery*. New York: Holt & Company, 1998.

Web Sites

International Save the Children Alliance
www.savethechildren.net
The International Save the Children Alliance Web site provides visitors with information on the organization's programs, campaigns, and operations. There are also links to Save the Children organizations from around the world.

Save the Children U.S.
www.savethechildren.org
At the Save the Children U.S. Web site, visitors can learn about the organization, become a sponsor, make a donation, or take action. Visitors can also follow Save the Children's activities in the news section.

Save the Children's Youth NOISE
www.youthnoise.com
Youth NOISE is a Save the Children initiative that works to inspire youths to help other youths through volunteering, fundraising, and speaking out. The youth NOISE Web site allows children and young adults to stay informed and share their opinions with others.

Glossary

AIDS: a disease that slowly destroys the body's natural ability to fight off other diseases; stands for acquired immune deficiency syndrome

charter: a document outlining rights or privileges for a group of people

developing countries: countries that are undergoing the process of industrialization

discrimination: unfair treatment of a person or group based on race, religion, or gender

exploitation: unfair treatment of someone for profit or personal gain

famine: a severe shortage of food causing widespread hunger

Great Depression: an economic collapse in the 1930s

maladjusted: unable to cope with everyday social situations and relationships

malaria: a disease carried by mosquitoes

midwives: people who are trained to help deliver babies

patron: somebody who gives their support to an organization

refugee: a person who has left his or her country, often because of war

sustainable: can be maintained

Index